Divine

CW00401744

A Tale of
Espionage and
Divine Protection

Pinchas Chalk

Contents

Chapter 1: Escape to Aliyah

"Yankel, are you sure about this?" Sarah Stempelhoffer questioned her husband, her voice layered with a mix of excitement and trepidation.

"Absolutely!" Yankel replied with a grin, trying to wrestle his battered Akubra hat into a cardboard box, where it jostled for space with his old engineering textbooks and mismatched pairs of socks.

"Aliyah, think about it - blue skies, a warm breeze, the Mir Yeshiva, and no more lockdowns. No more Dan Andrew's coronavirus regime!" His eyes twinkled at the thought of leaving behind the perpetual gloom of the past couple of years.

"But Yankel..." Sarah started, her eyes widening, "We don't speak Ivrit! And what about our jobs? What about the kids' schools?"

He paused, considering her point. Then with a chuckle, he said, "Well, Sarah, you have a choice. You can either live in the Land of Lockdowns, or in the Land of Milk and Honey, which one would you prefer?"

Sarah laughed. The past couple of years had

been challenging under the strict Australian coronavirus regime. The allure of a fresh start was indeed appealing. "I suppose the kids will enjoy the adventure. And you, Mr. Engineer, will surely find a job."

"Of course!" Yankel proclaimed. "And speaking of jobs, think of the wonderful opportunity we have to introduce our neighbours to the glory of Vegemite."

Sarah cringed at the thought, and Yankel erupted into laughter.

"Dan Andrews said the lockdown would only be for two weeks," Yankel began dramatically, pretending to be a news reporter. "Two weeks turned into two months, then two years! If this continues, I'll forget what the world looks like."

As the laughter died down, Yankel's gaze landed on a framed photo of a particularly chubby rabbit with glossy fur.

"You know, I'll miss Chaim Daryavesh Cocopops," he said, referring to their beloved pet rabbit that had recently passed away in traumatic circumstances (for Yankel).

"Me too," Sarah said. "Remember when he

chewed through your engineering notes?"

Yankel chuckled. "Oh yes, he had a taste for knowledge, that one. But I'm sure now, in Olam Habah he is crunching through an infinitely large field of carrots and lettuce."

Sarah grimaced and reminded herself not to let Yankel buy any more pets.

"Alright, Yankel. Let's go!" she said, determination lacing her words.

"Fantastic!" Yankel declared, throwing his arms up in celebration and knocking over a box of kitchen utensils. They both winced at the clatter.

"Maybe the Mossad will recruit you because of your stealth," Sarah joked, grinning.

"Who knows," Yankel said, adjusting his Akubra, "Maybe they will."

Little did they know that this jesting remark would soon turn into a reality far beyond their wildest imaginations. Their adventure was only beginning, and the road to their new life in Israel was lined with surprises, excitement, and a story they would never forget.

Chapter 2: Mossad Recruiters

The bustling Ben Gurion Airport was filled with the sounds of hurried footsteps, murmured conversations, and the ever-present hum of aeroplanes taking off and landing. Yankel, Sarah, and their children had just arrived, weary but filled with the excitement of starting their new life in Israel.

As Yankel pushed a cart loaded with luggage, he adjusted his Akubra hat, feeling both out of place and uniquely himself. It was a strange sensation, being in a new country but knowing that this was where he was meant to be.

"Welcome to Israel!" Sarah said, her eyes sparkling.

Yankel grinned. "Yes, welcome indeed.

Now, where did I put that map of the apartment?"

As he rummaged through his bags, he noticed a well-dressed man observing him from a distance. The man's eyes were hidden behind dark sunglasses, but his gaze was fixed squarely on Yankel's Akubra hat.

"Sarah, I think someone's watching us," Yankel whispered, his voice tinged with curiosity rather than fear.

Sarah glanced over and chuckled. "Maybe he likes your hat."

Yankel continued to watch the man, intrigued. The man approached, his stride confident and purposeful.

"Mr. Stempelhoffer?" the man asked, his accent crisp and professional.

"That's me," Yankel replied, still clutching the handle of the cart. "Can I help you?"

"I believe it is I who can help you," the man said, extending a hand. "I am known simply as The Handler."

"The Handler?" Yankel repeated, raising an

eyebrow. He shook the man's hand cautiously.

"Indeed. I represent a secret government organisation that has taken interest in your unique skills, particularly in the field of electrical and electronics engineering."

Yankel's eyes widened. "You mean the Mossad?"

The Handler's lips curled into a slight smile. "I see you're quick to understand. Yes, the Mossad."

Sarah's jaw dropped, and she looked at Yankel in disbelief. "You were joking about this back in Australia!"

The Handler continued, his voice calm and measured. "Mr. Stempelhoffer, we have a top-secret project that we believe you are uniquely suited for. A project that, if successful, will save Israel from a potential disaster."

Yankel's heart pounded in his chest. The thrill of adventure, the weight of responsibility—it was all so sudden, so overwhelming.

"But why me?" Yankel stammered. "I mean, I'm just an engineer from Australia who wears funny hats."

"The Akubra caught our eye," The Handler admitted, "But it's your engineering prowess that we need. We've been observing you for quite some time, even before your aliyah. Your skills are precisely what this mission requires."

Yankel glanced at Sarah, seeking reassurance. She nodded, her eyes filled with pride and concern.

"What would I have to do?" Yankel asked, his voice filled with determination.

"You'll be briefed in detail," The Handler explained. "But know that this mission is of the utmost importance. It's a matter of national security."

Yankel thought for a moment, his mind racing with questions and possibilities. The infinite carrot field, the promise of a new life, the adventure—it all seemed to converge at this singular point.

"I'm in," he said firmly, looking The Handler in the eye.

"Excellent," The Handler said, his face betraying a hint of relief. "Welcome to the

Mossad, Mr. Stempelhoffer. Your code name will be GRAPKE. It stands for 'Guidance, Readiness, Accuracy, Precision, Knowledge, and Engineering.'"

Yankel's heart swelled with pride, knowing that he was about to embark on a journey that was bigger than himself.

"Welcome to the team, GRAPKE," The Handler said, clasping Yankel's shoulder.

As The Handler departed, leaving Yankel with a small envelope containing further instructions, Yankel turned to Sarah, his eyes wide with excitement and awe. "We're not just in Israel, Sarah," he said, his voice filled with wonder. "We're in the Mossad!"

Sarah and Yankel wheeled their cart towards the exit, ready to embrace their new adventure.

The promise of blue skies, warm breezes, and the Mir Yeshiva awaited them, and Yankel knew that he was ready to face it all, Akubra firmly in place. The world of espionage had just gained a uniquely Aussie touch, and the Mossad's mission had found the perfect rabbit-loving electronics engineer to guide them to success.

Chapter 3: The Unseen Headquarters

The train's rhythmic clatter was hypnotic, lulling Yankel into a state of reflection as he gazed at the passing Israeli landscape. The Handler sat across from him, a steady presence, betraying no emotion or anticipation. The contrast between the normalcy of the train ride and the gravity of the mission ahead was surreal.

As the train approached Netania, Yankel's thoughts were interrupted by The Handler's abrupt movement.

"Get ready," The Handler instructed, his voice betraying no emotion. "We're getting off at the next station."

"The next station? But that's Bet Yehoshua. I thought we were going to Netania," Yankel said, confusion in his voice.

"We are," The Handler replied, a cryptic smile playing on his lips. "But not in the way you might expect."

As the train slowed to a stop at Bet Yehoshua, a small station in the countryside, The Handler led Yankel off the train. Yankel followed, feeling a mixture of curiosity and trepidation.

Over the railway bridge they walked, the air filled with the scents of earth and eucalyptus. Yankel noticed a grove of gumtrees, and The Handler led him toward it.

"Watch out!" The Handler suddenly yelled, pulling Yankel down to avoid a 600-volt cable cunningly strung between the trees.

"What's this about?" Yankel stammered, still in shock from the near miss.

"All in good time, GRAPKE," The Handler replied, using Yankel's new code name. "Follow me."

They continued through the grove, arriving at a green ramshackle shed that seemed entirely out of place. Yankel's mind raced with questions, but The Handler's demeanour encouraged silence.

As they entered the shed, The Handler moved to a dusty bookcase at the back and shifted it aside, revealing hidden stairs leading down.

"Welcome to Mossad HQ," The Handler said, gesturing for Yankel to follow him.

Descending into the underground headquarters was like entering another world. The place was bustling with activity. Agents, scientists, and support staff hurried to and fro, engaged in tasks that Yankel could only begin to imagine.

The Handler guided Yankel through the labyrinthine corridors, finally stopping at an imposing door.

"Before you begin your work, GRAPKE, there is someone you must meet," The Handler said.

The door opened to reveal a man whose very presence commanded respect and authority. He was known only as GRAMITZ, the enigmatic head of Mossad.

"Welcome, GRAPKE," GRAMITZ said, his voice as calm and measured as his demeanour. "We've been expecting you."

Yankel felt a chill run down his spine as GRAMITZ's eyes bore into his. He knew that he was in the presence of a man who had shaped the very destiny of Israel's intelligence community.

"We have great faith in you, Yankel,"

GRAMITZ continued. "Your mission is vital to our nation's security. We trust you will fulfil it with the honour and integrity we expect from our operatives."

With a firm handshake, Yankel was dismissed, his head reeling from the meeting. He was now part of something far greater than himself, and he knew that he had to succeed.

The Handler led him to his new base, a room marked "GRAPKE," furnished with a freezer containing mini ice-creams, a fridge containing a seemingly infinite supply of yoghourts, a laptop on a desk and the components of a cruise missile.

"This is your new office GRAPKE," said The Handler, "Enjoy!"

Chapter 4: The Hidden Threat

The Handler sat down with Yankel in Yankel's new office. His voice was grave as he said, "GRAPKE, we've intercepted a communication between two senior Hezbollah personnel. You need to hear this."

A crackle filled the room as The Handler played a telephone recording. General Yessir Areyoufat of Hezbollah was speaking.

***

"Colonel Armoured Dinnerjacket, the Iron Dome has rendered our rockets useless. Every time we shoot missiles at Israel they get shot down. We have to figure out how to beat the Israelis at their own game."

Colonel Armoured Dinnerjacket, another high-ranking Hezbollah officer, replied: "Indeed, General. Our best option is to develop cruise missiles that can evade detection by the Iron Dome system. But we lack the expertise to do this."

"We do?" replied General Yessir, "Well then let the Israelis do it for us."

"What???" replied Colonel Dinnerjacket.

"Well if we can't do it, then we're going to have to get the Israelis to do it for us, right?" replied General Yessir.

"What???" replied Colonel Dinnerjacket again.

"Why do you keep saying 'what'? What do you mean 'what'?" said General Yessir testily.

"I mean," said Colonel Dinnerjacket slowly, "Why on earth would the Israelis want to help us beat the Iron Dome?"

"They wouldn't," replied General Yessir, "But they're going to anyway.

We have recruited a German spy called Hans Dummkopf, he's going to set up a shell IT company in Jerusalem, recruit Israeli engineers to design the cruise missiles, and then send us the plans."

Colonel Dinnerjacket gasped at General Yessir's audaciousness.

"What will the shell company be called?" asked Colonel Dinnerjacket.

"It will be called Baalabatischer Ballistics, or The BB Company, for short."

"What does that mean?"

"I don't actually know," admitted General Yessir, "But I asked ChatGPT to suggest 20 names for our shell company and that was the most Jewish sounding one it came up with, so I'm going with that."

***

The recording ended, and the room was filled with a tense silence. Yankel's eyes were wide, his mind racing to comprehend the audacity of the plot.

"So, that's the plan," The Handler said, breaking the silence. "They're attempting to weaponize Israeli brilliance against us. Your mission, GRAPKE, is to infiltrate Baalabatischer Ballistics as an electronics engineer."

Yankel nodded, still stunned by the revelation. "I'll do whatever it takes."

The Handler leaned forward, his eyes intense. "Once you're inside, you'll need to do precisely nothing for the Mossad. Just be the best engineer they've ever hired. Do your job to the best of your ability."

Yankel frowned, perplexed. "Nothing? But then how will I beat their plan?"

"Further instructions will be forthcoming," smiled The Handler, and left the room.

***

The game was on, and Yankel was ready to enter the lion's den, wearing the disguise of an unsuspecting engineer. The world of espionage had become his reality, and he knew that the safety of his new home depended on his success.

But first he had to familiarise himself with cruise missile technology. Yankel worked through the night, trying to understand the electronics needed to guide a cruise missile on its deadly path. By the morning he understood all he needed to know.

Now Yankel was ready to face it all, his mind clear, his mission set, and his Akubra waiting to accompany him on this new adventure.

Chapter 5: The Interview at Baalabatischer Ballistics

Yankel awoke the next morning with a sense of purpose, a new challenge ahead. His resume had been adjusted to suit the requirements of Baalabatischer Ballistics, the BB Company, a promising technology firm in Jerusalem. Now, he was about to face the man behind it all, Hans Dummkopf, alias Professor Hermann von der Sauerkraut.

The building was sleek and modern, buzzing with creative energy. Yankel felt a surge of adrenaline as he was ushered into Professor von der Sauerkraut's office.

The Professor was tall and thin, with piercing pale-blue eyes that seemed to look right through Yankel. He wore a large head covering that looked more like an upside down salad bowl than a hat, and his glasses were cracked. Together this gave him a somewhat alien appearance.

The Professor's handshake was firm, his demeanour professional but slightly cold.

"Ah, Yankel, I've been looking forward to meeting you," the Professor began, gesturing for Yankel to sit. "Your qualifications are impressive, and your experience in electronics engineering is exactly what we need for our new project."

Yankel's heart pounded in his chest as he replied, trying to keep his voice steady. "Thank you, Professor. I'm eager to contribute to the BB Company's goals."

They dived into technical discussions, and Yankel's knowledge of cruise missile technology proved to be up to the task. The Professor was visibly impressed, nodding and asking in-depth questions.

But as the interview wore on, Yankel could sense something in the Professor's gaze, a hint of suspicion, a glimmer of doubt. Was it his imagination, or did the Professor sense something amiss?

Finally, the Professor leaned back in his chair, a thoughtful expression on his face. "Yankel, I must admit, your expertise is exactly what we're looking for. I'm inclined to offer you the position."

Yankel's heart leaped, but he kept his expression neutral. "Thank you, Professor. I'm honoured."

"However," the Professor continued, his eyes narrowing slightly, "I must ask, what drew you to the BB Company? Our project is quite unique, and I'd like to understand your motivation."

Yankel's mind raced, but he kept his cool, explaining his fascination with cutting-edge navigational technology and his desire to contribute to something innovative and groundbreaking.

The Professor's eyes searched Yankel's face for a moment longer before he finally smiled. "Very well, Yankel. Welcome to Baalabatischer Ballistics."

As Yankel left the office, elation mingling

with anxiety, he knew that the real challenge had just begun.

Later that day, the Professor sat at his desk, staring at Yankel's resume, his mind troubled. He picked up a secure phone and dialled a number known only to a select few.

"Hezbollah HQ," a voice answered.

"It's von der Sauerkraut," the Professor said, his voice betraying a hint of unease. "I've hired the new engineer. He's perfect for our needs, but something about him... I can't quite put my finger on it. I'll keep a close eye on him."

The voice on the other end was reassuring. "Do that, Professor. Trust your instincts."

As the call ended, the Professor's eyes lingered on Yankel's photo, a nagging doubt in his mind. He would have to be cautious. The stakes were too high to make a mistake.

The game of espionage had entered a new phase, and both sides were playing for keeps.

Chapter 6: A Close Brush with a Watermelon

Back at Mossad HQ, tension was building in the control room. The team had picked up Professor von der Sauerkraut's call to Hezbollah, and concern on their faces was palpable.

"What do you think, GRAMITZ?" one of the analysts asked, looking to the seasoned leader of the unit.

The GRAMITZ's eyes were narrowed, his mind clearly working through the possibilities. "He's suspicious of Yankel. If the Professor digs too deep, he might uncover Yankel's true identity. We can't risk that."

Another voice chimed in, belonging to an agent known only as X. "Then we must do something to divert his suspicion, something bold and unpredictable."

All eyes turned to X, an enigmatic figure with a reputation for unconventional thinking. X continued, "We should stage an assassination attempt on Yankel by dropping a watermelon on his head from a high-rise building. If the Professor believes that Mossad is targeting Yankel, he will be convinced that Yankel is not our man."

The room fell silent, the astuteness of the plan sinking in.

The GRAMITZ finally broke the silence. "It's risky, but it might just work. X, you'll handle the operation?"

X nodded, a steely determination in his eyes. "I'll do it."

"Good," the GRAMITZ said. "Make it look real, but ensure Yankel's safety at all costs."

The following day, Yankel was walking home from his first day at Baalabatischer Ballistics, still absorbing the complex dynamics of his new role. Unbeknownst to him, X was atop a nearby building, a ripe watermelon in hand.

The timing had to be perfect. The Professor had planted surveillance on Yankel, and they needed to be sure he would witness the attempt.

The building was approximately 240 metres tall, giving the watermelon a long descent to gather velocity. Ignoring air resistance, the watermelon would hit the ground at approximately 68.7 metres per second, releasing kinetic energy equivalent to about 14,000 joules, nearly the energy contained in a small stick of dynamite.

As Yankel walked beneath the high-rise, X let the watermelon plummet. Yankel looked up just in time to see the descending fruit and rolled away. The watermelon smashed into the ground where his head had been moments before, the energy released in a mini explosion of pulp and rind that sent Yankel flying through the air and landing a few metres away, shaken but unharmed.

Yankel's breath came in ragged gasps as he processed what had just happened. Who had tried to kill him with a watermelon? And why?

Meanwhile, the Professor was reviewing the surveillance footage, his mind whirling. Someone had dropped a watermelon on Yankel. Was it an accident, or was it the Mossad? If it was the Mossad, then that could mean only one thing: Yankel was innocent. He made a quick call.

"Hezbollah HQ," answered the impersonal voice.

"It's von der Sauerkraut again," said the Professor, "Someone dropped a watermelon on our new engineer. I don't know if this was an accident or the Mossad."

"Go figure it out yourself," said the impersonal voice, and hung up the phone.

Back at Mossad HQ, X debriefed the team. "The Professor is now in a state of doubt, I may need to have another go at Yankel to persuade him that we really are trying to eliminate his new engineer."

"OK X," said the GRAMITZ, satisfied but sombre. "But make sure Yankel stays alive."

The game of shadows continued, the stakes rising, and Yankel's role at the heart of it all, more critical than ever.

Chapter 7: Aussie Trousers

Yankel stumbled home, his mind reeling from the bizarre and unexpected watermelon attack. His clothes were covered in bits of watermelon, and he could feel the sticky juice drying on his skin. But, as he inspected his beloved Australian trousers, he was relieved to find them intact. The trousers had survived the ordeal without a single tear, a testament to their quality and indestructibility.

As he entered the house, Sarah's face went pale as she took in his watermelon-strewn appearance. "Yankel!" she cried, rushing forward. "What happened? Are you hurt?"

Yankel laughed, holding up his hands to show her he was unharmed. "I'm fine, I just had a close encounter with a falling watermelon. But the important thing is, my trousers are safe!"

Sarah stared at him, bewildered, then burst into relieved laughter. "Only you, Yankel, could come home after an attempted watermelon assassination and worry about your trousers!"

"They don't make them like this in Israel, Sarah!" Yankel protested, feigning seriousness.

"These trousers are irreplaceable!"

They laughed together, but as the laughter faded, Sarah's eyes filled with concern. "But seriously, Yankel, what's going on? Why would someone drop a watermelon on you?"

Yankel's smile faded as he considered the situation. His mind raced through the possibilities. Was it the Mossad? No, he was working for them. Was it The BB Company? But they'd just hired him, and he was critical to their project. The options seemed to cancel each other out, leaving him with nothing but uncertainty.

"I don't know, Sarah," he finally admitted, his voice tinged with concern. "It doesn't make sense. Why would Mossad want to kill me when I'm on their side? And why would The BB Company try to take me out when they just gave me a job? It's all very confusing."

Sarah watched him, her brow furrowed in thought. "Could it be someone else? Someone you haven't considered?"

Yankel shook his head. "I can't think of anyone else who would want to target me. It's baffling."

They sat in silence for a moment, the weight of the unknown threat hanging heavy in the room.

"I'll have to mention this to The Handler," Yankel said at last, his voice determined. "Maybe he'll have some insights."

Sarah nodded. "Just be careful, Yankel. If someone wants to take you out, you'll need to be on your guard."

"Don't worry," Yankel assured her, his mind already working on the next steps. "I'll be more careful in future. But for now, at least my Aussie trousers survived."

With that, they both managed a laugh, but the shadow of uncertainty lingered, adding a new layer of complexity to Yankel's already perilous mission.

Chapter 8: The Double Board Gambit

Yankel was still reeling from the inexplicable watermelon incident when he received a secure communication from his Mossad contact, known only as The Handler. The message instructed Yankel to meet in a discreet location that night, one that they had used for covert discussions before.

Upon arrival, Yankel found The Handler waiting for him, a serious expression on his face.

"GRAPKE, I've got a task for you," The Handler said, getting straight to the point. "Something very specific."

Yankel listened intently as The Handler explained the mission. The Handler's plan was both ingenious and puzzling. He wanted Yankel to persuade Professor von der Sauerkraut that the cruise missiles' accuracy would be improved if each cruise missile had two GPS boards instead of one.

Yankel looked at The Handler, curiosity piqued by the mission's technical intricacy.

"Before we proceed, can we discuss the technology behind this? I want to fully understand the purpose of the GPS board in a cruise missile and how the implementation of two would actually function."

The Handler nodded, recognizing the value in ensuring Yankel's comprehension. "Certainly, GRAPKE. A GPS board is the component that tells the navigation brain of a cruise missile where the missile is currently located.

It's the hardware that interfaces with the Global Positioning System, pinpointing the missile's location in real-time as it moves toward its target."

Yankel nodded, listening intently. "Right, and by using the GPS data, the missile can correct its course, adapting to any deviations from the planned trajectory."

"Exactly," The Handler replied. "The GPS board constantly receives signals from satellites, calculating the missile's position and velocity. It feeds this data to the navigation computer, which makes real-time adjustments to the missile's flight path, keeping it on target."

"So why two boards?" Yankel asked, getting to the crux of the mission. "What's the engineering advantage?"

The Handler leaned in, his eyes intense. "By having two independent GPS boards, we introduce redundancy. If one board fails or experiences interference, the other can take over, reducing the risk of a total navigation failure."

"But there's more to it," Yankel said, his mind racing with the possibilities. "By taking the average of the readings from both boards, we could potentially filter out noise or any inconsistencies. Even if both boards are functioning correctly, there might be slight variations in their readings. Averaging these could yield a more accurate position."

The Handler's eyes sparkled with approval. "Precisely, GRAPKE. You've grasped the concept perfectly. This approach could lead to better precision, especially in environments where the signal might be compromised or where there's a risk of intentional jamming."

Yankel's eyes widened at the thought. "So we're not just improving the system; we're also enhancing its robustness against potential countermeasures."

The Handler smiled. "Exactly. It will seem like a substantial improvement to the Professor, and he'll likely embrace it."

"But I don't understand," Yankel said, his brow furrowed in confusion. "Why are we trying to help the Professor improve the missile system? What's the end game here?"

Before The Handler could respond, Yankel continued, "And what about the watermelon attack? Was that also part of the mission?"

The Handler's eyes narrowed, and he looked around once more to ensure privacy. "The watermelon was a distraction, GRAPKE. A cover-up to get the Professor off guard. You see, we needed the Professor to believe that we are a threat to you, so that he should believe you're not our agent."

Yankel blinked, taking in the revelation. The Handler's plan was brilliant but terrifying in its complexity.

"I see," Yankel finally said, his voice subdued. "This is more complicated than I thought."

The Handler placed a reassuring hand on Yankel's shoulder. "That's why we chose you, GRAPKE. We trust you to handle it."

Yankel nodded, determination replacing his initial shock. "I'll do my best."

"And what about the improvement to the missile guidance system," asked Yankel, "Why am I going out of my way to help the Professor?"

"That's not for you to know, GRAPKE," said The Handler. Your job is to carry out the mission. The reasons behind it are on a need-to-know basis, and right now, you don't need to know."

Yankel looked at The Handler, sensing the gravity of the situation. He trusted the Mossad, trusted that they were working for the greater good, even if he didn't understand all the pieces of the puzzle.

"OK," he said firmly, committing to the task.

"Good," The Handler replied, a hint of relief in his voice. "I knew I could count on you."

As Yankel left the meeting, he couldn't

shake a growing sense of unease. The mission was clear, but the motives behind it were murky. He was being asked to walk a tightrope without knowing what awaited him on the other side.

But he knew one thing for certain: He was in deep, and there was no turning back. The dance of deception and intrigue was becoming more intricate, and Yankel was at its core, a pawn in a game he could not fully comprehend.

Chapter 9: The Olive Oil Deception

Professor von der Sauerkraut sat at his desk, his fingers drumming impatiently on the surface as he pondered Yankel's proposition. While the idea of adding a second GPS board to the missile system was undeniably appealing, he couldn't shake the nagging doubt that Yankel might be an undercover agent.

He picked up the phone, dialling the secret Hezbollah number that he used only for the most sensitive communications. On the other end, a voice answered.

"Speak," the voice commanded, its tone cold and unyielding.

"It's me," the Professor said, anxiety

creeping into his voice. "I've been approached with a proposition to improve our missile guidance system. It's promising, but the engineer behind it—I'm not sure if he's to be trusted."

"You still think he's a spy?" the voice on the other end asked, interest piqued.

"I don't know. Something doesn't feel right," the Professor admitted. "What if this is a trap? What if the Mossad are trying to manipulate us?"

"Hold on, I'll need to consult with others," the voice said before the line went dead.

Unbeknownst to the Professor, his phone call was being intercepted by the Mossad. Listening intently, The Handler recognized the Professor's apprehension as an opportunity to further their agenda.

"We need to convince him that Yankel is not our agent," The Handler told his team, his eyes gleaming with determination. "We'll stage another assassination attempt. Something subtle, something that could be easily explained away but will also put Yankel's life in jeopardy."

"What do you have in mind?" one of the agents asked.

"Olive oil," The Handler replied, a sly smile spreading across his face.

***

Yankel was riding to work, enjoying the early morning breeze on his face as he navigated the city streets. He came to the street The BB Company was located on, and approached the roundabout just before the building he worked in.

Unbeknownst to him, two people were carefully watching his progress.

The Professor was watching him, wondering how far he could be trusted, and X was watching from a distance, carefully timing the release of olive oil that was dripping from his backpack onto a roundabout just ahead.

As Yankel entered the roundabout, he tried to turn. He felt a sudden loss of traction, his bike slipping and sliding uncontrollably. The next thing Yankel knew he was sliding across the roundabout on top of his bike. A car screeched to a halt inches away from him, as he finally came to a stop.

His heart pounding, Yankel pulled his bike to the side of the road, his mind racing. This was no accident; someone had tried to kill him.

At a distance, the Professor mentally concurred with Yankel and concluded that he was innocent. They would adopt Yankel's double GPS board plan.

He made a quick call to Hezbollah HQ to explain what had happened, and then thoughtfully sipped the coffee that had grown cold waiting for him to drink it.

Back at Mossad headquarters, The Handler watched the footage of the staged accident, satisfied that their plan had gone off without a hitch.

"The Professor will believe that Yankel is our target now," he said to his team, his eyes narrowing with resolve. "We have tightened the net around our quarry."

Chapter 10: Bandages and Cream

Yankel's fall had left him with only minor scratches and sores, but he had decided to take no chances. On the way home, he stopped at the pharmacy and bought an entire backpack full of creams, bandages, and plasters. He even threw in a first-aid manual, just in case.

He burst through the door of his small flat, his face flushed with excitement, his arms filled with shopping bags.

"Sarah!" he called, his voice full of urgency. "I've been attacked! But don't worry, I have everything we need!"

Sarah emerged from the kitchen, her face full of concern. "Attacked?" she exclaimed. "What happened? Are you okay?"

"I'm fine, I'm fine!" Yankel assured her, setting down his bags and beginning to unpack. "Just a minor scrape. But you can never be too careful! Look at all these creams! And these bandages! And these plasters!"

He held up a particularly large roll of bandages, his eyes shining.

Sarah stared at him, her mouth agape.

"Yankel, where are we going to keep all of this? Our flat is tiny! And... are you sure you need all that for a small scrape?"

Yankel looked at her, his eyes wide with disbelief. "Of course I do! Haven't you read about infection? And scarring? And and other... other things?"

He trailed off, suddenly unsure.

Sarah couldn't help but laugh. She went over and took the bandage roll from him, setting it down on the table.

"You're overreacting," she said gently, her eyes twinkling. "A little soap and water will do the trick. You're not dying, you know."

Yankel looked at her, then at the pile of supplies, then back at her. Finally, he grinned sheepishly.

"Maybe I did go a little overboard," he admitted. "But it's better to be safe than sorry!"

Sarah shook her head, still smiling. "Only you would turn a bike fall into a shopping spree. Come on, let's get you cleaned up."

***

They managed to cram everything into a cupboard, where it would likely gather dust until the end of time. But Yankel didn't mind. He felt safe, knowing that now he was prepared for anything that would come his way.

Chapter 11: The Bargain with Zhao Mingxing

The breakthrough came when Mossad's cyber unit managed to intercept The BB Company's order for GPS boards on AliExpress.

Sifting through the digital paper trail, the team traced the order to a specific factory on the outskirts of Shenzhen, China. The owner, a man named Zhao Mingxing, was known in tech circles for his cutting-edge products but had no known connections to the global game of espionage that was rapidly unfolding around his business.

X's task was clear. The seasoned agent was to fly to China and negotiate a clandestine modification to the GPS boards, paving the way for the Mossad's master plan.

The flight to China was uneventful, and X used the time to study the intricacies of the planned mission. He had 20 diamonds as clandestine payment. The diamonds were certified by the Gemmological Institute of America, each one a stunning one carat Pink Argyle, valued at $500,000. They were the bargaining chips in a high-stakes game that was about to unfold.

Zhao Mingxing's factory was nestled among a maze of industrial buildings, seemingly innocuous. Yet within its walls lay the key to the next phase of the Mossad's strategy.

Zhao was waiting, having been contacted by an anonymous source promising a lucrative business proposition. The meeting was set in his lavishly decorated office, adorned with art reflecting his refined tastes.

As X entered, Zhao rose, extending a hand with a friendly smile. "Welcome, my friend. I am Zhao Mingxing. How may I help you today?"

X's eyes were cold but not unfriendly, his voice measured. "Mr. Zhao, I have a proposition for you—one that could prove mutually beneficial."

Zhao's eyes narrowed slightly, intrigued.

"I'm listening."

X laid out the plan, detailing the backdoor that needed to be added to the GPS boards. It had to be discreet, undetectable, and activated by an encoded radio signal containing the ID of the GPS board and a secret code. When triggered, it would offset the output of the GPS by 200 kilometres east, a tool with immense potential in the hands of Mossad.

Zhao's face was inscrutable as he listened, but X could see the gears turning in his mind. He knew the value of what was being asked and the complexity of the task.

"Why would I do this?" Zhao finally asked, his voice betraying no emotion.

X reached into a briefcase and produced five Pink Argyle diamonds, letting them catch the light, their sparkle and colour a silent testament to their worth.

Zhao's eyes widened, but he quickly regained his composure. "This is indeed a generous offer. But why should I trust you? What if the authorities find out?"

X's smile was thin. "We have our ways, Mr. Zhao. Your involvement will remain a secret."

Zhao sighed, his face softening. "Fees for Melbourne Grammar School, where I send my children, have recently become astronomical, due to Dan Andrews' new tax on private schools. This offer is indeed tempting."

X could see that he had him. The personal motivation, combined with the substantial reward, had sealed the deal.

"Very well," Zhao said, extending his hand. "We have an agreement."

X shook it, his grip firm. "A pleasure doing business with you, Mr. Zhao."

As X left the factory, he knew that a crucial piece of the puzzle had fallen into place. The stakes were high, but the rewards were even higher.

With the successful completion of this critical step, the game of shadows continued, each move more daring than the last, the world's future delicately hanging in the balance.

Chapter 12: The Basel Kirsch Heist

The project was nearing its crescendo, the pieces aligning, and the stakes growing ever higher. Baalabatischer Ballistics' development had brought Hezbollah's entire arsenal of 70,000 rockets in Lebanon to the brink of cruise missile capability. The urgency in Mossad's operations was palpable.

Yankel, now deeply embedded within the BB Company, was summoned to a secret meeting with The Handler, the shadowy figure who guided Yankel's every move within the organisation.

"You've done well, GRAPKE," The Handler said, his voice tense but pleased. "But now we're entering the final and most critical phase. We need to acquire the ID of every GPS board installed in each missile. It's all on the Professor's laptop."

Yankel's eyes widened, the weight of the task settling upon him. "How do you suggest I do that?"

The Handler's smile was thin, his eyes calculating. "I've done some research, GRAPKE. Our dear Professor has a weakness for Kirsch from Basel, a particular brand of

Swiss cherry brandy. We're going to exploit that weakness. You'll invite him to celebrate the project's success and then... encourage him to indulge."

Yankel raised an eyebrow, a hint of concern in his eyes. "Get the Professor drunk? That's the plan?"

The Handler's gaze was unwavering. "Exactly. Once he's inebriated, you'll have the opportunity to access his laptop. Our cyber team will guide you through the extraction process. Timing and execution will be everything."

Yankel took a deep breath, absorbing the audacity of the plan. He knew the Professor well enough by now to know that the man did, indeed, have a fondness for Swiss cherry brandy. But could he really get him drunk enough to access his laptop without arousing suspicion?

"I understand the risks," Yankel finally said, his voice steady. "I'll do it."

The Handler nodded, satisfied. "Good. We've arranged for a shipment of the Professor's favourite Kirsch. You'll find it at a safe location. Details are in this envelope."

He handed Yankel a sealed envelope, their eyes meeting in a silent understanding. This was it—the moment when all their careful planning would either pay off or unravel in catastrophic failure.

The days that followed were a blur of preparation and tension. Yankel managed to secure a private dinner with the Professor, his invitation laced with just the right amount of flattery and enthusiasm. The Professor, pleased with the progress of their work and trusting in Yankel's loyalty, readily agreed.

The night of the dinner arrived, and Yankel's heart pounded in his chest as he welcomed the Professor to his home, the Kirsch from Basel prominently displayed. A toast was made to their success, and the evening unfolded according to plan.

As the Professor's laughter grew louder and his speech more slurred, Yankel's mind raced, the moment of truth approaching.

Back at Mossad HQ, The Handler watched the live feed, his fingers drumming on the desk. The success of the entire operation hinged on

Yankel's performance in these next crucial hours.

Chapter 13: Of Fingerprints and Spreadsheets

With the Professor deep in a Kirsch-induced slumber, Yankel's heart pounded as he approached the Professor's laptop. The mission was clear: access the machine, locate the spreadsheet containing the IDs of the GPS boards, and send them to The Handler. Yankel felt the weight of Mossad's expectations bearing down on him.

Carefully, he opened the laptop, trying to recall the glimpses he had caught of the Professor's password. His fingers flew over the keys, and a moment later, the screen prompted for a fingerprint.

Yankel's breath caught in his throat. A fingerprint! He hadn't anticipated this layer of security. Panic bubbled within him, but he forced it down, focusing on the task at hand. The Professor was asleep in the next room, and his fingerprint was the key.

With a glance at the security feed on his phone, ensuring the Professor remained asleep, Yankel carried the laptop into the dimly lit room where the Professor was snoring softly. The smell of Basel Kirsch lingered in the air.

Carefully, oh so carefully, Yankel reached down and lifted the Professor's hand. He felt the pulse of the man's life beneath his fingers, aware of the fragility of the moment. He pressed the index finger onto the fingerprint reader, praying that the Professor would remain asleep.

A soft chime sounded, and the laptop

unlocked.

Yankel's breath whooshed out in relief, and he returned to the study, his mind racing. He quickly located the required spreadsheet, the data he sought spread across multiple pages. The seconds ticked by, each one a tiny eternity as he considered his options. He couldn't copy the file directly; the Professor would detect that. He needed another way.

Inspiration struck, and he pulled out his smartphone, carefully photographing each page of the spreadsheet. The images were clear and crisp, every detail captured. He attached them to an email and sent them to The Handler, his heart in his throat.

A soft chime from his phone confirmed the receipt, and Yankel's legs nearly gave out in relief.

Back at Mossad HQ, The Handler opened the email, the images of the spreadsheet spreading across his screen. They had it! The critical data, the key to their entire operation, was now in their hands.

He quickly sent a message to Yankel, the words simple but filled with meaning. "Well done."

Yankel read the message, a sense of pride mingling with the lingering adrenaline. He had done it. His mission was a success.

As he carefully closed the laptop and returned it to its place, the enormity of what he had just accomplished began to sink in. He had breached the defences of one of the most secretive and dangerous organisations on Earth, and he had come out victorious.

But the game was far from over, and Yankel knew that the real battle was only just beginning. The stakes were higher than ever, and he was at the centre of it all, a player in a shadowy game where the fate of nations hung in the balance.

As he finally settled into sleep that night, Yankel knew that he had crossed a line, and there was no going back. The world had shifted, and he was now a part of something much larger than himself, a cog in a machine that would stop at nothing to protect its people.

Chapter 14: Secret Talks in London

London's Hilton Hotel had seen its fair share of notable guests and distinguished events, but on this particular night, it played host to a meeting that would not make the history books. In one of the hotel's secure conference rooms, a tense negotiation was underway, with the fate of a fragile peace hanging in the balance.

Representing Israel was Nir Ben-Ari, a seasoned diplomat with a reputation for shrewdness and resolve. Across from him sat Hassan Nasri, Hezbollah's envoy, a man equally known for his cunning and tenacity. Both had been chosen for their ability to navigate the treacherous waters of international politics, but the chasm between them seemed unbridgeable.

"You know our demands," Nasri began, his voice cold and calculated. "The air-raids by the Israeli Air Force on Iranian targets in Lebanon must stop. The sovereignty of Lebanon is non-negotiable."

Ben-Ari's eyes narrowed, his expression unreadable. "You speak of sovereignty, but what of the Iranian installations? What of the threat they pose to our nation? You must understand our position."

"Your position?" Nasri spat, his composure slipping for a moment. "Your actions are an affront to our dignity. You act as if Lebanon is your playground, disregarding international law."

"International law?" Ben-Ari shot back, his voice rising. "Where is the law when rockets are aimed at our cities? Where is the law when Iranian forces operate freely on your soil?"

"The matter of Iran is not the subject of these talks," Nasri said, his voice regaining its icy control. "We are here to discuss the air-raids, nothing more."

"And we cannot discuss the raids without addressing the reason for them," Ben-Ari countered, his tone equally firm. "The threat to us is real, Nasri, and you know it. If you want the raids to stop, you must address the root cause."

Nasri's eyes flashed, but his voice remained steady. "And what assurances do we have that you will uphold your end of the bargain? How can we trust you when you violate our borders at will?"

"Trust is built through action," Ben-Ari said, leaning forward, his gaze unflinching. "Give us a reason to stop the raids, and we will."

"And how do you propose we do that?" Nasri asked, his tone mocking. "Hand over our sovereignty to you?"

"You know that's not what we're asking," Ben-Ari replied, his voice controlled but filled with conviction. "But you must take concrete steps to address the threat to us from Iran. Only then can we talk of peace."

The room fell into silence, the tension palpable. Both sides knew the stakes, and both knew that the path forward was fraught with danger.

Finally, Nasri broke the silence. "We will consider your words," he said, his voice heavy with the weight of the decision. "But know this: our patience is wearing thin. The air-raids must stop, one way or another."

With that, he stood, signalling the end of the meeting. Ben-Ari watched him go, his mind already turning to the next steps.

The negotiations were on the brink, and the future was uncertain. The fate of a region hung in the balance, and the choices made in that room would echo far beyond the walls of the Hilton.

As the door closed behind Nasri, Ben-Ari allowed himself a moment of reflection. The path ahead was unclear, but one thing was certain: the game of shadows was far from over, and the next move would be critical.

Chapter 15: Nuclear Shadow

Inside a secure briefing room at the Israeli Intelligence Directorate, a small group of high-ranking officials and military officers were assembled. The atmosphere was fraught with anxiety as General Eitan Cohen, head of the Directorate, began the briefing.

"Ladies and Gentlemen," Cohen started, his voice grave. "We have received credible intelligence that Iran is installing nuclear-tipped weapons in Lebanon. This is not a drill or mere speculation. The evidence is irrefutable."

He clicked a remote, and the large screen behind him displayed satellite images of a facility in the Bekaa Valley, near the town of

Zahle. The images were incredibly detailed, revealing not just the external structures but also the internal workings of the site.

"This facility," Cohen continued, "has been under our watch for some time. Initially, we believed it to be a standard missile installation site. But recent intel has uncovered something far more sinister."

The images on the screen zoomed in to show a series of underground bunkers, guarded by advanced air defence systems. There were also glimpses of what appeared to be missile silos, large enough to house ballistic missiles.

"The geolocation coordinates are 33.8471° N, 35.9042° E," Cohen specified. "These bunkers are being used to store and possibly launch Shahab-3 ballistic missiles, which are capable of carrying nuclear warheads."

He then switched to another image, this time a close-up of a specific section of the facility. It showed technicians working on a missile, fitting it with what looked unmistakably like a nuclear warhead.

"The Shahab-3 has a range of 2,000 kilometres and is capable of carrying a payload of up to one ton. If equipped with a nuclear tip, the devastation it could cause is unimaginable. The technical precision of this operation is astounding. The Iranians are using specialised loading vehicles and advanced crane systems to ensure secure handling of the warheads."

The room was silent as the implications of the information sank in.

Defence Minister Yossi Kfir finally broke the silence, his voice trembling with concern. "What options do we have, General? This changes everything."

"We have already begun mobilising our Iron Dome and Arrow missile defence systems," Cohen replied. "But we must also consider a pre-emptive strike. The risk is enormous, but the alternative is unthinkable."

Prime Minister Avner Herzog leaned forward, his face etched with determination. "We must act decisively, but we must also be cautious. This is not just a threat to Israel but to the entire region. We must work with our allies and ensure that we have international support."

The meeting continued late into the night,

with debates, strategy sessions, and careful planning. Every detail was scrutinised, every possibility explored.

The shadow of a nuclear Iran had been cast over the Middle East, and Israel found itself at the epicentre of a crisis that could redefine the geopolitical landscape. The game of shadows had taken a dark and dangerous turn, and the choices made in the coming days would reverberate across the world.

The stakes had never been higher, and the path forward had never been more fraught with peril. The clock was ticking, and time was running out.

Chapter 16: The President's Dilemma

In the elegant confines of the President's Office, President Reuven Adler sat behind his ornate desk, his face a mask of concentration as he listened to Prime Minister Avner Herzog and General Eitan Cohen outline the harrowing situation.

"Gentlemen, please take your time and explain this to me clearly," President Adler said, leaning back in his chair. "I need to understand every aspect of this crisis."

Prime Minister Herzog began, his voice measured but filled with urgency. "Mr. President, as we have discovered, Iran is actively installing nuclear missiles in Lebanon. The satellite images and on-ground intelligence leave no room for doubt. We are facing an existential threat."

He paused, letting the weight of his words sink in before continuing.

"Our military experts, including General Cohen, have determined that a massive air strike is our most viable option to neutralise these missiles. However, such a move would undoubtedly provoke a response from Hezbollah."

General Cohen took over at this point, his voice steady but his eyes betraying the gravity of the situation.

"Hezbollah's missile arsenal is estimated at 70,000, and they are distributed across Lebanon," Cohen explained. "If we launch an airstrike, they will likely retaliate by firing these missiles simultaneously at Israel. Our air defences would be totally overwhelmed."

President Adler's eyes narrowed as he

considered the dire scenario. "But that's not all, is it? You mentioned something about cruise missile capabilities?"

"Yes, Mr. President," Cohen confirmed. "Our intelligence suggests that Hezbollah's missiles have been upgraded with cruise missile capabilities. This means that they are now far more accurate, versatile, and difficult to intercept. The shell BB Company has been working on this technology, and it appears they have succeeded."

The room fell into a heavy silence as the magnitude of the problem became clear.

"So, let me get this straight," President Adler said, his voice filled with disbelief. "If we strike Iran's nuclear missiles in Lebanon, Hezbollah will unleash a barrage of missiles on us, potentially causing massive devastation. And if we don't act, we leave ourselves vulnerable to a nuclear attack from Iran. Is that the situation?"

Herzog and Cohen exchanged glances before Herzog answered, "Yes, Mr. President. That's the situation."

President Adler stood up and walked over to

the window, staring out at the cityscape, his mind racing. The decisions he faced were monumental, with consequences that could alter the course of history.

After a long moment, he turned back to his advisors.

"Gentlemen, we must explore every possible option, every diplomatic channel, every military strategy. We cannot act rashly, but we cannot afford to delay. Convene the National Security Council. Bring in our best minds. We will work around the clock if we have to."

He paused, his eyes filled with determination.

"We will find a way through this. We must."

Chapter 17: Operation Leviathan's Breath

A shadow of terror had fallen upon the nation of Israel. Secret information had reached the highest echelons of the Israeli government, confirming Iran's plan for a nuclear strike. Time was no longer a luxury, and the situation called for immediate and decisive action.

At the Defence Ministry:

In a secure room at the Defence Ministry, General Cohen convened an emergency meeting with his top military commanders and intelligence officials. The blueprints for a massive aerial raid were unfurled on the table, and the atmosphere was one of grim determination.

"Ladies and Gentlemen," Cohen began, his voice steady but filled with urgency, "Operation Leviathan's Breath is now in motion. We are targeting Iran's nuclear missile installation in Lebanon, and we must act swiftly."

He turned to the maps and detailed plans, highlighting the key targets and strategies.

"All air bases across the country are on high alert. We will perform a massive simultaneous strike, with waves of fighter jets, bombers, and drones. Precision and coordination are key. Every second counts."

The room listened intently, aware of the historical weight that rested on their shoulders.

"We also need to prepare our home defence," Cohen continued. "Intelligence has warned that 70,000 Hezbollah cruise missiles could be coming our way soon. We need to be ready for every scenario."

At the Israeli Air Bases:

As the plans were discussed and refined, air bases across Israel buzzed with activity. Fighter jets were armed, pilots briefed, and every element of the military machine primed for action.

At Ramat David Airbase, Squadron Leader Amir was addressing his pilots. His face was stern but confident, his words chosen with care.

"We are tasked with hitting the heart of the installation," he said, looking into the eyes of his men and women. "Our mission is to neutralise the threat and get out safely. I know you are the best, and I trust you."

At Hatzerim Air Base, Captain Baruch gathered his team around him. He understood the gravity of the mission, and his voice carried both authority and empathy.

"This is not just another sortie. We are defending our nation, our families, and our future. Let's make sure we give it everything we have."

Across the country, pilots huddled around briefing tables, studying maps, memorising targets, and going over the mission details. The weight of their task was heavy, but their resolve was unbreakable.

Home Defence Preparations:

Simultaneously, the Israeli Home Defence was put on high alert. The missile defence systems, Iron Dome, David's Sling, and Arrow 3 were tested and retested, their operators drilled for the worst-case scenario.

Shelters were prepared, emergency services coordinated, and citizens were given discreet warnings to be prepared for any eventuality.

The Calm Before the Storm:

As the sun set on a tense and anxious day, Operation Leviathan's Breath was set in motion. The eyes of the nation and the world were fixed on a small strip of land in the Middle East, where destiny was being shaped.

Israel was ready to strike, but it knew that the repercussions could be catastrophic. The choice had been forced upon them, and they could only pray that their actions would bring security rather than unleashing a storm of unimaginable proportions.

In the shadows, unseen players watched and waited, knowing that the game had reached its climax, and the next move would determine the fate of nations. The pilots said their goodbyes, the mechanics made their final checks, and the nation braced itself for a historic conflict.

Chapter 18: Dawn of Vengeance
4:00 AM - Israel's Skies:

As the first rays of dawn were yet to pierce the horizon, a thunderous roar filled the air across Israel. Operation Leviathan's Breath had begun.

A fleet of fighter jets, bombers, and support aircraft soared at supersonic speeds, creating shockwaves that shook the ground beneath them. People were startled awake, their hearts pounding, as they stumbled from their beds and ran to air raid shelters, their minds racing with confusion and fear.

In the air bases, the ground crews watched as the last of the planes took off, their eyes filled with a mixture of pride and anxiety. They knew that the success of the mission lay in the hands of their pilots, and they could only wait, hope, and pray.

The Bombardment – Iran's Nuclear Missile Installation:

In the darkness of the Lebanese hills, the target lay hidden, an underground lair that housed a deadly arsenal. The Israeli forces approached with stealth and precision, their instruments locked onto their objectives.

Then, without warning, the night sky was lit up by a barrage of missiles, bombs, and laser-guided munitions. The destruction was immediate and overwhelming.

The earth shook violently as a local earthquake erupted from the sheer force of the bombardment. The ground above the underground missile facility cracked and crumbled, swallowing the entire installation in a chaos of rock and fire.

The once-secret nuclear missile site was

reduced to rubble, the threat neutralised in a relentless assault that left no room for doubt or survival.

Hezbollah's Response:

The shockwaves of the attack reverberated throughout the region, reaching the ears of Hezbollah's leadership. The vow for revenge was immediate and fierce.

A secret code was sent to all Hezbollah terror cells in Lebanon, a directive that left no ambiguity. The order was to launch a simultaneous missile strike on Israel at 6:00 AM, a response that would rain terror and destruction upon the Jewish state.

The cells activated, the missiles were prepared, and a countdown to vengeance began.

Israel's Home Front:

Back in Israel, the uncertainty and tension were palpable. The thunderous sounds of the departing jets had given way to an eerie silence, broken only by the distant rumble of air defences being prepared.

Families huddled in shelters, children clung

to their parents, and everyone waited, not knowing what would come next. The news of the successful attack had not yet reached the public, and fear mingled with hope in the hearts of millions.

The government and military were on high alert, aware that the response from Hezbollah could be swift and devastating. Plans were in motion, defences were ready, but the shadow of 70,000 cruise missiles loomed large, a threat that could not be taken lightly.

As the clock ticked towards 6:00 AM, the eyes of the world were fixed on a region on the brink, a place where the battle lines had been drawn, and where the stakes were higher than ever.

Chapter 19: The Moment of Truth

5:59 AM - The World Waits:

As the last seconds ticked away, the world held its breath, gripped by a tension that was almost palpable. The news had spread, and the eyes of nations were fixed on Lebanon and Israel, waiting for what could be a pivotal moment in history.

In capitals and homes, leaders and citizens

alike stared at screens, waiting, praying, fearing. The seconds seemed to stretch into hours, a moment frozen in time as destiny teetered on a knife-edge.

6:00 AM - Lebanon's Skies:

With the strike of the hour, the skies of Lebanon were ignited with the fiery trails of 70,000 cruise missiles, each on its deadly course towards cities, towns, and villages across Israel. A sea of destruction was unleashed, a storm of terror that would spare nothing in its path.

In the command centres of Hezbollah, a grim satisfaction settled over the faces of those who had orchestrated the launch. Revenge was at hand, and they were the bringers of chaos.

Mossad Underground HQ:

In the bowels of Mossad's secret headquarters, the tension was unbearable. The GRAMITZ, along with X and the rest of the elite team, stared at a radar screen now filled with a terrifying white mass representing the oncoming missiles.

The room was filled with a silence that was both heavy and expectant, the weight of a nation's fate resting on their shoulders. The

GRAMITZ's hand hovered over the red button that would send the secret code to corrupt the output of the second GPS on every cruise missile.

He pressed it.

They waited.

Nothing happened.

The terror in the room was immediate, a cold dread that settled into the pit of their stomachs. Faces turned pale, hands shook, and the realisation that their plan had failed began to sink in.

All were frozen in horror, except for X.

A flash of memory, a moment of clarity, and X's eyes widened. The radio transmitter's output had been shorted to earth via an incandescent lightbulb for testing, a safety precaution that now threatened disaster.

Without a word, X bolted from the room, his mind focused, his body driven by a singular purpose.

The rest of the team could only watch, their eyes still fixed on the radar screen, their minds grappling with the unthinkable.

Time was running out.

The Race Against Time:

X's footsteps echoed through the corridors as he ran, his heart pounding, his thoughts filled with the knowledge that every second counted.

The RF switch room loomed ahead, the place where the fate of millions could be decided with a single action.

He reached the door, flung it open, and rushed to the panel. The incandescent lightbulb glowed ominously, a symbol of failure that he would not accept.

With a swift motion, he switched the RF output to the radio transmitters, a simple action that carried the weight of history.

He paused for a moment, his breath ragged, his eyes filled with hope and determination.

Back in the control room, the GRAMITZ and the team waited, their eyes still fixed on the radar screen, their hearts in their throats.

Would it work? Had they done enough?

The answer would come soon, and with it, the fate of a nation.

Chapter 20: Neriah's Bonus Catch
6:05 AM - Off the Coast of Tel Aviv:

Neriah was a simple fisherman. His father had been a fisherman before him, and his father's father before that. Fishing was in his blood, a calling that connected him to the sea and the traditions of his family.

He always liked to get an early start, believing that the early morning hours were when the sea revealed its bounty. By 6 AM, he was usually in the middle of the sea off the coast of Tel Aviv, just before dawn, when the world was still and the fish were plenty.

But today was different.

As he settled into his usual routine, casting his nets and preparing for a peaceful morning, he noticed something strange. The early morning sky seemed brighter than normal, a glow that was out of place and filled him with a sense of confusion.

He scratched his head bemusedly and looked up, his eyes widening as his face turned white.

Tens of thousands of lost cruise missiles were streaking across the sky, heading directly towards him. Their fiery tails lit up the horizon, an apocalyptic sight that filled him with terror and awe.

Time seemed to slow as the missiles approached, their roar growing louder, their presence an undeniable reality that he could neither escape nor comprehend.

He could only watch as they shot over his boat, a swarm of deadly projectiles that were now nothing more than lost wanderers of the sky. They seemed to dance and weave, their paths unpredictable, their destinations unknown.

And then, as quickly as they had come, they were gone, plunging into the sea with thunderous impacts that sent waves crashing around his boat.

Neriah's heart was pounding, his mind struggling to grasp what had just happened. He was alive, untouched by the chaos that had unfolded around him.

But the surprises were not over.

As the sea calmed and the missiles sank into the depths, Neriah noticed something extraordinary. His nets were filled with fish, a bumper catch that was unlike anything he had ever seen.

Fish, knocked unconscious by the impact of the cruise missiles, had floated to the surface, a gift from the sea that he could never have imagined.

He looked around, the reality of the morning sinking in, the enormity of what had just happened washing over him.

He was alive, his boat was intact, and he had a catch that would feed his family for weeks.

A smile slowly spread across his face, a realisation that he had witnessed a miracle, a moment in time that was both terrifying and beautiful.

He looked to the heavens, offering a silent prayer of thanks, and then turned back to his work, a fisherman once more, forever changed by a morning that would become a legend in his town.

The world had teetered on the brink, but for Neriah, life would go on, guided by the rhythms of the sea and the wisdom of generations.

It was a day he would never forget, a story he would tell for the rest of his life, a tale of survival and serendipity that was as incredible as it was true.

Chapter 21: The Explanation

11:00 AM - President's Office, Jerusalem:

The President of Israel sat at his desk, a look of relief mixed with curiosity on his face. Across from him were Yankel, the GRAMITZ, and X, the heroes of the hour, the minds behind the miraculous diversion of 70,000 cruise missiles.

The President looked at them, his eyes reflecting gratitude and a thirst for understanding. "Gentlemen, I cannot begin to express my gratitude for what you have accomplished today. But I must know, how exactly did you manage to divert those missiles into the sea? What was the science behind it?"

Yankel cleared his throat, a diagram of the dual GPS system on the screen behind him. "Mr. President, the success of our operation lies in the use of two GPS boards in each cruise missile, and the manipulation of their outputs.

Allow me to explain."

He pointed to the first GPS board on the diagram. "This board works as it should, providing the correct positioning data."

Then, he pointed to the second. "This board, however, has been engineered with a backdoor, allowing us to adjust its output by 200 kilometres east, when receiving a specific encoded signal."

The President leaned forward, intrigued. "Go on."

X picked up the explanation. "When the cruise missile's navigation computer averages the output of both GPS boards, it figures out it is 100 kilometres to the east of where it is meant to be according to its flight plan. Therefore it flies 100 kilometres to the west to compensate for this discrepancy."

"The result," X continued, "in practical terms, is that the missile will land exactly 100 kilometres to the west of the target it was meant to land on, which in Israel's case means that it will land in the middle of the sea."

The President concentrated. "So, by compromising the output of one GPS board, you've turned the missiles away from their intended targets, sending them harmlessly into the ocean," he asked.

"Exactly, Mr. President," the GRAMITZ confirmed, his face reflecting pride in their achievement. "It's a precise manipulation, executed with exacting care."

The President seemed satisfied but then raised another concern. "But couldn't the missile's navigation computer directly interrogate the GPS board, asking it to confirm its odd reading? Wouldn't that reveal the manipulation?"

Yankel looked at X, who took the lead in answering this complex question.

"Mr. President, that's an insightful question, and it's precisely why we implemented the dual GPS board strategy. Normally, the navigation computer could directly query the GPS board. However, in this case, the navigation computer was not receiving output directly from either of the GPS boards."

He pointed to the diagram on the screen. "You see, we introduced an averaging program in between the GPS boards and the navigation computer. This program took the outputs from both boards, the normal one and the altered one, and then averaged them before passing the data to the navigation computer."

Yankel continued, "This created a layer of separation between the navigation computer and the GPS boards. The computer was only able to interact with the averaged data, not the individual GPS boards. Therefore, it couldn't interrogate a specific board to confirm its reading."

The President's eyes widened as he realized the depth of the plan. "So you essentially put a 'firewall' between the GPS boards and the navigation computer, ensuring that the computer could never detect the manipulation. That's incredibly ingenious."

The GRAMITZ nodded. "Indeed, Mr. President. It was a delicate balance, requiring precise coordination and timing. Any discrepancy could have been detected, but by controlling the data flow and masking the manipulation, we were able to guide the missiles off course without raising any alarms."

The President leaned back in his chair, clearly impressed by the strategic brilliance of their approach. "Gentlemen, your plan was not just a technological triumph; it was a masterclass in strategic thinking. The nation owes you a great debt."

They exchanged respectful nods, understanding the magnitude of what they had accomplished.

"Thank you, Mr. President," Yankel replied, his voice filled with humility. "We were honoured to serve."

They knew that their success was a testament to *siyata di'shmaya* and their unyielding commitment to their country's safety.

As they left the President's office, they carried with them a sense of fulfilment, knowing that they had risen to the challenge and emerged victorious. Their trust in Hashem had prevailed, turning potential disaster into a triumph over their enemies.

The President watched them go, a smile on his face, grateful for their brilliance and proud of their unwavering loyalty. They were the unsung heroes of a nation, their victory a symbol of Jewish endurance and ingenuity.

Chapter 22: The Professor's Reward
3:00 PM - Hezbollah HQ, Lebanon:

The Professor strode into Hezbollah's headquarters, his eyes gleaming with satisfaction and anticipation. He was expecting praise and a handsome reward for his successful work on the cruise missiles.

General Yessir Areyoufat, Hezbollah's top official, was waiting in his office. His face was contorted with rage, a bottle of Kirsch in one hand, the same kind that Yankel had used to intoxicate the Professor earlier.

Unaware of the true situation, the Professor extended his hand with a confident smile. "Yessir Sir, it's a pleasure to see you. Our project has been a tremendous success."

Yessir's eyes widened, his face turning crimson. "Success? SUCCESS?" he roared, hurling the bottle of Kirsch at the Professor, who barely dodged it.

"What's going on?" the Professor stammered, confusion and fear in his eyes.

"You fool!" Yessir screamed, his voice dripping with fury. "Your precious cruise missiles fell into the sea! They were worthless! All that time, all that money, all that effort, and for what? A bunch of fish! And to top it all off, you allowed yourself to get drunk on this very bottle of Kirsch and gave away our secret GPS codes!"

The Professor's face paled as the reality sank in. His legs carried him around the room, Yessir's furious shouts echoing in his ears.

"I trusted you! I believed in you! And you've failed me!" Yessir's voice was a thunderous roar, his pursuit relentless.

After a wild chase, Yessir's men finally managed to restrain their leader, his face red and his eyes wild with fury. The Professor was cornered, his heart pounding, his mind racing.

"I want him gone," Yessir spat, his voice dripping with contempt. "Package him up and send him back to where he came from."

His men grabbed the Professor, who struggled and pleaded, his world collapsing around him. They stuffed him into a large trunk, sealing it shut.

A label was slapped onto the trunk: "Express Courier to Mossad HQ, Bet

Yehoshua."

The package was hauled away, the Professor's muffled cries echoing through the hallways of Hezbollah's headquarters.

Yessir watched it go, his face still twisted with anger. He had been deceived, outmanoeuvred, defeated. He looked down at the bottle of Kirsch in his hand, its contents now a bitter reminder of his failure.

He hurled it against the wall, the glass shattering, the liquid splattering.

The room was left in silence, the only sound the dripping of the Kirsch, each drop a symbol of a dream crushed, a plan foiled, a battle lost.

In his heart, Yessir knew that this was the end. His plans, his dreams, his power—all destroyed by a simple bottle of Kirsch and the incompetence of a man he once trusted. The feeling of betrayal and loss weighed heavily on him, a burden that would not easily be forgotten.

The war was over, and he had lost.

Chapter 23: A Promise Fulfilled
10:00 AM - Mir Yeshiva, Jerusalem:

The smell of old *sefarim* and polished wood filled the air as Yankel stepped into the vast *beis hamedrash* of Mir Yeshiva. It had been a long and harrowing journey, filled with danger, intrigue, and unexpected twists. But now, he was home. He felt an inner peace that had been absent for far too long.

The Yeshiva was filled with the sound of learning as *talmidei chachamim* studied, their voices rising and falling in a rhythmic cadence. Yankel was drawn to a side room where the Mashgiach was delivering a *mussar schmooze*, an ethical discourse that delved into the depths of the soul.

Yankel found a seat among the students, his

heart swelling with anticipation. The Mashgiach was a wise and learned man, known for his profound insights and ability to connect timeless wisdom to current events.

"My dear students," the Mashgiach began, his voice resonating with warmth and authority, "we have witnessed a miracle, a divine intervention that has once again shown us the hand of Hashem in our lives."

The room was silent, the students leaning in to hear every word.

"Hezbollah's entire cruise missile arsenal, a weapon designed to wreak havoc and destruction upon our people, has been neutralised in one miraculous stroke. Seventy thousand missiles, all rendered useless, falling harmlessly into the sea."

A murmur of awe swept through the room.

"The *neviim* spoke of Hashem's eternal promise to protect the Jewish people in Eretz Yisrael forever. Today, we have seen that promise fulfilled before our very eyes."

Yankel's heartbeat with a powerful realisation. He had played a part in this miracle, an instrument in Hashem's divine plan.

"We must not take this *nes* for granted," the Mashgiach continued, his eyes filled with fire and conviction. "We must recognize it for what it is: a call to return to Hashem, to deepen our connection to Him and to live our lives in accordance with the Torah."

The words resonated with Yankel, touching him to the core of his being. The mission, the intrigue, the danger—all of it had led him to this moment of profound understanding.

The *schmooze* ended, and the students dispersed, their faces thoughtful, their hearts filled with renewed faith and determination.

Yankel remained seated, lost in thought, the words of the Mashgiach echoing in his mind. He had been part of something greater than himself, a divine orchestration that had brought safety and security to his people.

As he left the Yeshiva, he looked up at the clear blue sky, feeling a profound connection to Hashem and a renewed sense of purpose.

He knew that he was not alone, that Hashem's guiding hand was always with him, and that he was part of an eternal covenant that would never be broken.

With a heart full of gratitude and a soul at peace, Yankel walked into the bright Jerusalem sun, ready to face whatever lay ahead, knowing that he was part of a timeless promise, a divine plan that transcended the here and now.

The End.

Printed in Great Britain
by Amazon